Brown Rabbit's Shape Book

Alan Baker

SCHOLASTIC INC.

New York Toronto London Auckland Sydney

ISBN 0-590-63089-X

Copyright © 1994 by Alan Baker.
All rights reserved under International and Pan-American Copyright Conventions. Published by Scholastic Inc., 555 Broadway, New York, NY 10012 by arrangement with Larousse, Kingfisher, Chambers, Inc., New York.

12 11 10 9 8 7 6 5   5 6 7 8 9/9

Printed in U.S.A.   14

First Scholastic printing, September 1994

One day a package arrived
for Brown Rabbit.
It had bright red triangles
on the wrapping paper.

The card was
the shape of a
rectangle. It said
"To Brown Rabbit."

Rabbit took off the paper.
Underneath was a
square box. Rabbit
lifted the lid.

Inside was
a tube ...

... with a circle shape top.
Rabbit opened it.

Out tumbled
five flat floppy
balloons,
all different
colors.

Lovely balloons,
just waiting
to be blown up.

Rabbit blew up the red balloon.
It was big and round like a ball.

Whoosh! It flew off.

The orange balloon was
oval-shaped like an egg.

Whoosh! Away it flew.

The green balloon was l o n g
and sausage-shaped.
Rabbit couldn't hold it.
Whoo-whoosh!
Off it went.

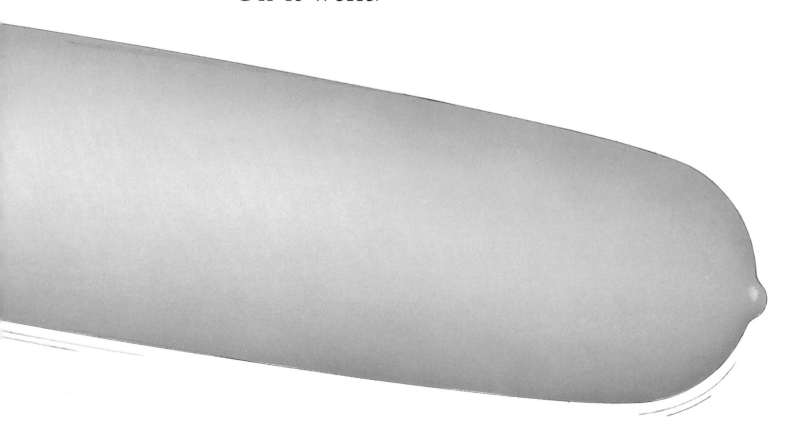

The purple balloon
was smaller and
shaped like a pear.

One more puff, thought Rabbit.
Then BANG! It burst.

The last balloon was all colors,
l o n g and curly-wurly.

Whoosh! Blast off!

Whoo ... Whoo ... Whoo-oosh!

Goodbye, balloon shapes.
I'm all out of puff,
thought Rabbit.

He tidied up the balloons,
the tube, the box,
and the paper.

Then rabbit-shaped Rabbit
fell fast asleep on top.